Harriet Bean
and the League of Cheats

Also by Alexander McCall Smith

Alexander McCall Smith

Harriet Bean
and the League of Cheats

Illustrated by Laura Rankin

BLOOMSBURY
CHILDREN'S
BOOKS

Published by Bloomsbury U.S.A. Children's Books
175 Fifth Avenue, New York, NY 10010
Distributed to the trade by Holtzbrinck Publishers

The Library of Congress has cataloged the hardcover edition as follows:
McCall Smith, Alexander.
Harriet Bean and the League of Cheats / by Alexander McCall Smith ;
illustrations by Laura Rankin. —1st U.S. ed.
p.   cm.
Sequel to : The five lost aunts of Harriet Bean.
Summary: Harriet helps her detective aunts, Thessalonika and Japonica,
investigate cheating at the racetrack by disguising herself as a jockey.
ISBN-13: 978-1-58234-976-3 • ISBN-10: 1-58234-976-2 (hardcover)
[1. Aunts—Fiction. 2. Horse racing—Fiction. 3. Mystery and
detective stories.]
I. Rankin, Laura, ill. II. Title.
PZ7.M47833755Ha 2006   [Fic]—dc22   2005031521

ISBN-13: 978-1-59990-054-4 • ISBN-10: 1-59990-054-8 (paperback)

Typeset by Hewer Text UK Ltd, Edinburgh
Printed in the U.S.A. by Worzalla
3 5 7 9 10 8 6 4 2

For Angus, Fiona, Alexandra,
Hamish, and Fergus

Contents

A Call for Help

Do you remember who I am? My name is Harriet Bean, and I was the person who had five lost aunts. Yes! It sounds ridiculous—perhaps even a bit careless—to have five lost aunts, but my father had never told me about them, and I had to find them all by myself. It was very hard, but I finally found every last one of them.

There was Aunt Veronica, who was a strong lady in a circus. There was Aunt Majolica, who was a very bossy teacher but really quite nice in spite of it. There was Aunt Harmonica, who was an opera singer who could also throw her voice into all kinds of places. And last of all, hidden away in their detective agency, there were Aunt Japonica and Aunt Thessalonika. They were very curious aunts with extraordinary tricks up their sleeves, and they could also read what was going on in other people's minds. What a marvelous collection of aunts!

When I said good-bye to my aunts after a wonderful reunion party, I knew that I was going to have adventures with them. It was a funny feeling—the kind of feeling that you have in your bones that something is going to happen. I had it the day they left, and the day afterward, and the day after that too. Then it happened, and because I had been expecting it, I was not in the least surprised.

The telephone rang early that morning. I think it was a Wednesday, because that was the day my father's favorite magazine arrived. He read *Inventors' Weekly*, which was all about the latest inventions, with tips for inventors, which is what he was. He wouldn't speak to me for hours after *Inventors' Weekly* arrived; he'd just sit in his chair, his nose buried in the magazine, giving the occasional snort. Sometimes I heard him say something like, "That would never work!" or "The screw's in the wrong place there!" or, very rarely he might say, "What a splendid idea! I wish I had thought of that first!"

I knew that my father would never answer the telephone while he was reading his magazine, so I did so myself. And at the other end of the line was Aunt Japonica.

"Harriet?" she said in her high, squeaky voice.

"Aunt Japonica," I said. "I'm glad it's you."

"Yes," said Aunt Japonica, in a business-like way. "You may be. And *I* certainly am glad it's *you*. We need your help."

My heart gave a leap of excitement. So this is what the thing was—the thing that I had known was going to happen.

Aunt Japonica did not talk for long. She asked me to come to the detective agency (where they also lived), if possible, within the hour. I put my hand over the receiver and shouted out to my father, to ask him whether I could go.

"Hmm!" he said from behind *Inventors' Weekly*. "Another no-tears onion peeler! I invented that years ago!"

"Can I go see Aunt Japonica?" I shouted.

"Japanese?" he snorted. "Did you say Japanese? Yes, of course. Very good at inventing things, the Japanese."

"I think he said yes," I explained to Aunt Japonica.

"Good," she said. "We shall see you very soon. And do hurry. There is something very, very odd going on."

Aunt Japonica and Aunt Thessalonika lived in a large studio at the top of a long flight of stairs. On the door there was a sign that simply said PRIVATE DETECTIVES, and underneath that was a bell. I pressed the button and heard, a long way off, a bell ringing.

Several minutes passed. Then the door opened slowly, and I saw an old man peering out at me. He seemed very ancient and very bent, and he had a walking stick in each hand.

"I'm so sorry," he said in a very old, cracked voice. "No, there's nobody in today. They've all gone away. All of them."

My mouth dropped open.

"B-b-but," I stuttered, "they knew I was coming. I spoke to them . . ."

The old man peered at me and shook his head. Then, with a sudden cackle of laughter, he jumped up in the air and clicked his heels together. For a moment or so I was too surprised to think, but then I realized what was happening.

"Aunt Thessalonika!" I exclaimed. "I had no idea it was you."

"Of course you didn't, my dear," said Aunt Thessalonika, taking my arm in hers and leading me down the corridor. "Sometimes I even fool myself. Do you know, the other day I was heavily disguised and I saw myself in the mirror. And I said to myself, 'Who are you, and what are you doing here?' Of course, the person in the mirror said exactly the same thing, and so I replied, 'But I'm Thessalonika and I *live* here!' And it's only when I heard the person in the mirror saying that she was Thessalonika that I realized what was happening."

As she spoke, Aunt Thessalonika removed layer after layer of disguise. Off came the gray beard. Off came the lines and the wrinkles, wiped quite clean, and there, underneath it all, was my aunt.

Aunt Japonica now appeared. At least *she* looked the same as she had the last time I saw her.

"Thank you for coming, Harriet," she said immediately. "And I see that you have been writing in your diary."

Once again, my mouth fell wide open with astonishment. She was right—I *had* been writing in my diary when she telephoned to invite me over. But how did she know?

Aunt Japonica gave a little laugh. "If you look at your right hand," she said, "you will see that there is an ink stain on the forefinger. Now that shows you have been writing. And what are you likely to have been writing? It's school vacation, is it not, so you will not be doing school work. You could be writing letters, but then when I called, you answered the telephone immediately. People who are writing letters never like to leave what they're saying until they've finished the sentence. Why is that? Well, it's obvious, isn't it? People feel it's rude to cut off halfway through a sentence when you're writing to somebody. Don't ask me why, but that's the way it is. Diaries are different. It's not rude to stop talking to yourself halfway through, is it?"

"No," I said, still astonished at how my detective aunts managed to work things out. That's what made them good detectives, I imagined.

We sat down for tea, and while Aunt Thessalonika cut the cake, Aunt Japonica explained why they wanted to see me.

"We could tell that you were interested in detective work," she explained.

"We could tell that from the moment we met you," chipped in Aunt Thessalonika.

"Yes," said Aunt Japonica, and then, from the side of her mouth, "please concentrate on what you're doing, Thessalonika. Cutting cake is not an easy task."

Aunt Japonica turned back to me and fixed me with her gaze. "You see," she went on. "A case has cropped up that we thought you might help us solve. After all, you are not as old as Aunt Thessalonika and I are. And you are somewhat smaller too. You can go where we can't go. You can, I imagine, run faster than we can, and your eyes might be a little better when it comes to detecting very fast movements."

"In other words," interrupted Aunt Thessalonika, "you might be able to catch these wicked cheats!"

Disguised!

Wicked cheats?

I sat back and listened as Aunt Japonica talked. Every so often, Aunt Thessalonika interrupted her to correct some detail or add a scrap of information. But for the most part, it was Aunt Japonica's story.

"We first heard about it only two weeks ago," she said. "We received a visit from a very famous trainer of racehorses. Now, do you know anything about horse racing?"

"No, she doesn't," interjected Aunt Thessalonika, fixing me with a piercing look. She was right, of course.

"Well, anyway," went on Aunt Japonica. "Racehorses have to be trained, and the people who do it are racehorse trainers. They take the horses for long gallops in the fields and teach them to go faster and faster. Then, when the horse goes into a race, it knows to gallop as fast as it possibly can. And that's all there is to it."

"Oh," I said. It did not sound very interesting to me, but I suppose that the horses enjoyed it.

Aunt Japonica took another sip of tea. Then she went on to explain that the trainer, Mr. Fetlock, had not won a race for over three months. All of his horses, which were normally very fast, had become very slow. One of them had even sat down in the middle of a race. Another had thrown its rider off even before the race had begun. Mr. Fetlock had no idea what the trouble was, but it was obvious that somebody was interfering with the horses in some way.

It sounded very simple to me. If somebody was interfering with the horses—perhaps by putting thorns under their saddles or sleeping pills in their oats—surely the answer was to watch and see who was doing it. I could not see how I could possibly help. Then Aunt Japonica answered my question.

"I see that you're wondering how you can help," she said, glancing at Aunt Thessalonika as she spoke.

Aunt Japonica looked at me closely.

"Have you ever seen the people who ride racehorses?" she asked. "Have you ever seen a jockey?"

I scratched my head. I thought that I had seen pictures of them in the newspapers. They wore riding helmets and very colorful shirts.

My aunts did not give me time to reply.

"They're smaller than most adults," Aunt Japonica said, her eyes glinting with enthusiasm. "Small people are lighter, and this allows the horses to go faster. So jockeys are usually not tall and certainly never fat."

"Yes," agreed Aunt Thessalonika. "They're really all . . . well, just about your size!"

Immediately, I knew why my aunts wanted me to help them on this case. But what exactly would I be asked to do, and would it be dangerous? Would I have to ride a horse? Worse still, would I have to enter a horse race?

That very afternoon I traveled with my two aunts out to Mr. Fetlock's racing stables. Mr. Fetlock himself met us at the gate and walked us up the long driveway to the group of buildings where the horses lived. He was a tall man, wearing brown jodhpurs, a smart checked coat, and riding boots.

"It's very good of you to come out here," he said. "I lost another race yesterday. It was my very best horse, Black Lightning. Not only did he come in last, but the horses in front of him overtook him on their second time around the racetrack. I was so embarrassed, I went and sat in my stall so that nobody would see me."

"Somebody's cheating," said Aunt Japonica through pursed lips. "If there's one thing I can't stand, it's a cheat."

"Yes," said Mr. Fetlock sadly. "But who can it be? The only people who have been anywhere near that horse over the last week are the stable boys and the jockeys themselves."

"I see," said Aunt Japonica thoughtfully. "Well, it must be one of them."

Mr. Fetlock looked astonished. "But that's impossible!" he snorted. "They wouldn't cheat me!"

Aunt Japonica shook her head. "We'll see about that," she said. "But first, would you please show us the place where you keep all the riding clothes? You know, jodhpurs, boots, jackets—things like that."

Mr. Fetlock looked puzzled, but, shaking his head, he led us to a small building near the stables. Unlocking the door, he pointed to a large cupboard against the wall.

"There's an awful lot of stuff in there," he said. "You could dress ten jockeys with that."

"We need to dress only one," said Aunt Japonica, opening the cupboard. She raked around inside, extracted some clothes, and passed them to me.

"If you'll wait outside, Mr. Fetlock," she said, "we will join you in a moment."

I looked at the clothes. Then I looked at my aunts, who smiled and nodded. With their help, and with a lot of pinning and tucking from Aunt Thessalonika, I was soon ready. Then, with a flourish, Aunt Japonica opened the door and we went out to join Mr. Fetlock. He looked at me in astonishment, and then his face burst into a wide grin.

"Harriet!" he cried out. "Or should I call you *Harry*? You look like a perfect jockey! Well done, my boy!"

Black Lightning's Stall

"**D**on't worry," said Aunt Japonica in a soothing voice. "You won't have to ride a racehorse. Will she, Mr. Fetlock?"

I swallowed hard. It was all very well dressing up as a jockey, and I think I looked like one, but what if somebody asked me to get up on a horse? It's not that I hadn't ridden once or twice before; it's just that there was every difference in the world between the small pony I had been on and the big race-horses I could see watching us from their stalls in Mr. Fetlock's stables.

Aunt Japonica drew me aside.

"We're going to leave you now," she

whispered. "Then, when the others come back from their afternoon ride, Mr. Fetlock will tell them that you're a new jockey who's come to work here."

I nodded. That part of the plan seemed simple enough, but what would happen after that?

"But what do I have to do?" I asked my aunt, wondering whether it was too late to say that I had changed my mind and that I wanted to go home.

"Really, Harriet!" said Aunt Japonica impatiently. "If you want to be a detective, you'll have to use your imagination. Just do what all the other jockeys do and see who's up to no good. Then you let us know. We'll be staying with Mr. Fetlock in his house over there."

"Will I be staying there too?" I asked.

Mr. Fetlock had overheard my question, and he laughed.

"Oh, no," he said. "I'm afraid all the jockeys have little rooms next to the horses. You can have the room next to Black

Lightning's stall. Very comfortable. A bit smelly, perhaps, but jockeys don't mind!"

"So you see," said Aunt Japonica, "it's all worked out. Now off you go to your room and wait for the others to come back. They'll be here in no time!"

For the first time since I had found all my aunts, I felt really miserable. As I sat on the edge of my bed in the little room next to Black Lightning's stall, I could hear my companion next door, scraping at his trough, his hooves tapping on the stone floor. I realized that I had made a terrible mistake. If only I had told my aunts that I was too busy to help them, or if only I had refused to get into the jockey's clothes, then I would not be sitting in this dark little room, waiting for something to happen.

There was a knock at the door. I looked up and saw a small person peering through my doorway.

"Are you Harry?" he said cheerfully. "Mr. Fetlock just told us there's a new jockey."

I stood up and walked over to the door-way, making sure that my hair was still tucked safely into my riding helmet.

"Er . . . yes," I said hesitantly. I would have to be careful to remember my new name, or I could easily give myself away.

"I'm Ted," said the jockey. "And that's Fred over there, and Ed's just getting a bucket of water."

I looked in the direction he was pointing. Fred waved to me, and Ed nodded in my direction as he came around the corner with his bucket.

"Well," said Ted, wiping at his brow with a rather dirty old cloth, "it's time to groom the horses. Are you ready?"

"Of course," I said, trying to make my voice sound as deep as I could.

"You'll need these," he said, tossing me a large brush and a strong metal comb. "You look after Black Lightning, and I'll do the one next door."

I stood outside Black Lightning's stall. The large racehorse, shiny black and curious, stared out at me. His nostrils were flared, and his breath came in deep heaves, as if two big bellows were pumping away within his chest.

I edged the door open and began to go into the stall.

"Now don't be frightened, Black Lightning," I said, holding out my hand to him. "I'm not going to hurt you."

This was ridiculous, of course. I couldn't possibly hurt Black Lightning, who was ten times my size; but he could hurt me—very easily. The horse watched me nervously, his large yellow eyes fixed on every movement I made. Slowly I lifted up the brush and pushed it toward him.

It was this movement that disturbed him. With a sudden whinnying noise, he rose up on his hind legs, his forelegs raised to strike at me. I fell back, trying to escape the heavy hooves that seemed to be falling all around me. Just behind me, set against one of the walls, was his trough, and I scrambled my way to safety under it. Black Lightning struck the ground a few more times, then stopped.

I was perfectly safe in my hiding place, as Black Lightning's hooves would never be able to reach me there. But I was also trapped, and as long as the racehorse was in his stall, it would be impossible for me to get out. I could try to crawl, I supposed, but the horse would easily be able to crush me if I did that.

I lay very still, wondering what to do. If I called for help, I was sure that Ted, Fred, or Ed would hear me, but what would they think if they found me hiding under a trough? They would realize at once that I was not a real jockey, and that would be the end of that.

The minutes ticked past slowly. Black Lightning moved a little, but I felt that he was still watching me, and I did not dare attempt to escape. Then, quite suddenly, I heard footsteps outside. I froze. If only it were Mr. Fetlock, or, even better, if only it were one of my aunts!

Slowly the door of the stall was pushed open.

"Hello in there," said a voice. "Anybody there?"

I said absolutely nothing. It sounded a bit like Ted's voice, but then again it sounded a little different. Could it be Fred, or even Ed?

I now saw boots coming into the stall. From where I was hiding, that was all I could see. I looked at the boots. They were ordinary riding boots, badly scratched at the back, just above the heels.

"Keep calm, boy," said the voice as the boots moved toward Black Lightning. "This isn't going to hurt you."

I wriggled as close as I could to the edge of the trough. Now I could see a little bit more—boots and a pair of legs mostly, but there was something else. There was a hand, and it was holding something that glinted. For a moment I could not make it out. Then I realized that it was a pot of something, with a brush sticking out of the top.

I held my breath as I watched what was happening. The person—whoever he was— had now run his hand down one of Black Lightning's legs and lifted up the hoof, as you

see people doing when they put on a new horseshoe or pick out a stone. Taking the brush out of the pot, he slapped paste of some sort on the hoof and put it down on the ground. Then he moved to the other side of the horse and did the same thing again. Within a few minutes he had put the paste on all of Black Lightning's four hooves.

"That'll fix you for a while," he muttered, and then, with a chuckle, the boots walked out of the stall, and the door was quietly closed.

I lay there for a while, wondering what I had seen. Somebody had certainly done something unpleasant to Black Lightning, but what was it? The horse seemed to be standing quite still and was certainly making no noise, so it could not have been anything painful. I slid forward again and peered out.

When Black Lightning saw my face peeking out from under his trough, he gave a start. Once again, his nostrils flared and his eyes shone with anger. I drew back slightly, expecting him to rear up and strike out at me again, but—to my astonishment—all he did was shake. For some reason, it seemed as if he was stuck to the spot.

I moved again. This time I stuck a leg out. Black Lightning watched it and shook his head from side to side. But once again, although all his muscles seemed to ripple and quiver with effort, his feet stayed exactly where they were.

Suddenly I realized what had happened. I had thought that Black Lightning was stuck to the spot. Well, he was! Black Lightning could not lift his hooves because the paste that had been put on them by the mysterious person in the riding boots was a powerful glue!

I now knew that it was safe for me to crawl out, and I did this. Black Lightning watched every move I made, but he was powerless to do anything about it. I left the stall quickly and went back into my room. There I lay down on my uncomfortable bed and thought about what I had seen. Why would anybody stick Black Lightning's hooves to the floor? And, even more importantly, *who* had done this peculiar thing? Was it Ted, Fred, or Ed? And how could I possibly find out?

At the Races

I was woken the next morning by the sound of Mr. Fetlock's voice outside my door.

"Time to get up," he called. "We'll be leaving for the races in half an hour. No time to waste."

I leapt out of bed and climbed into my jockey clothes. It was hard work putting on the riding boots, as boots like that are always tight, but at last I succeeded and made my way out into the yard. I wanted very much to talk to Mr. Fetlock—to tell him what had happened and to warn him that Black Lightning's hooves were stuck to the floor of his stable—but the trainer was busy talking to Ed and Fred.

I picked up a bucket of oats that looked as if it needed to be carried somewhere, but at just that moment, Ted came around the corner, and to my absolute astonishment I saw that he was leading Black Lightning! So the hooves had become unstuck overnight, or even been unstuck by somebody while I lay sleeping next door. It was all very mysterious.

"Hey!" shouted Ted. "Leave those oats, please. They're for Black Lightning. He's got a big race ahead of him today."

Mr. Fetlock looked over in my direction.

"Get into the truck with the other jockeys, Harry," he called out. "We've got a long drive ahead of us."

So I would not have the chance to warn Mr. Fetlock about what had happened. Still, I thought, I might be able to speak to him about it later, if I managed to get him by himself. Or I could tell my aunts. But where were they? There was no sign of them in the truck.

I climbed into the cab of the truck with Mr. Fetlock and the other jockeys. The horses had already been loaded into the back, and now that Black Lightning was also on board, we were free to leave.

"We've got three runners today," Mr. Fetlock said as he started the engine. "Fred, I want you to ride Silver Streak. Ted, you ride Nifty Dancer, and, Ed, you're on Black Lightning again. Harry, you just watch today."

"Right-oh, boss," said Fred. "That suits me. Silver Streak's due for a win."

"All my horses are due for a win," sighed Mr. Fetlock. "I can't understand why they've been losing so badly. Can any of you?"

I glanced from under my helmet at the faces of the three jockeys, wondering whether one of them would give himself away as the cheat. People often go red in the face if they're trying to hide something, but not one of them moved a muscle.

It could have been any of them, I thought. Ted looked honest, though. He had a cheerful grin on his face, and he smiled nicely whenever I looked at him. I wasn't so sure about Ed, and when it came to Fred, well, there was something about him that I just did not trust.

He looked a little bit like a rat, I'm afraid to say, with sharp teeth at the front of his mouth and little whiskers growing out of his ears.

I tried to look down at the boots that everybody was wearing. Perhaps if I saw the pair of boots again more closely, I might recognize the scratches, which I had noticed above the heel. Just as I was thinking this, an idea came to me. If I dropped something, a coin perhaps, I would be able to have a better look at everybody's boots.

"Excuse me," I said suddenly. "I think I dropped some money on the floor of the cab."

"Then pick it up," said Mr. Fetlock jovially. "There's nothing down there to bite you."

I leaned forward and began to scramble around on the floor of the cab. As I did so, I looked closely at the boots. Whose were those? Ted's. But were they at all scratched? No. He had just polished them, as had Ed and Fred. So everybody was going to the races in freshly polished boots. There was no

possibility, then, of working out whose legs I had watched in Black Lightning's stall.

The journey seemed to pass very quickly. In no time at all, Mr. Fetlock was swinging the large horse truck into the racing grounds. As the truck came to a halt, Ted and Fred jumped out and opened the back door. Then, while Ed held the door, the two jockeys led the horses out and tied them securely to a nearby railing.

I stayed near Mr. Fetlock, hoping to have the opportunity to talk to him, but one of the other jockeys always seemed to be at his side. Eventually I gave up. Perhaps it wasn't so important after all. I glanced down at Black Lightning's hooves; there was nothing wrong with them, as far as I could make out. Perhaps gluing them to the floor of the stable was just some sort of practical joke among the jockeys.

The time came for the first race. This was the race in which Silver Streak was entered, and in good time Fred was up in the saddle, ready to make his way to the starting gate. I walked across to the railings with Mr. Fetlock and Ed, and together we watched the horses line up for the start.

The starter's pistol took me by surprise and made me jump. Ed looked at me sideways.

"You should be used to that by now," he said suspiciously.

"Oh, he is, aren't you, Harry?" Mr. Fetlock blurted out jovially, trying to cover up for my mistake. "It's just that he had a little accident with a starter's pistol once, didn't you, Harry?"

"Oh?" said Ed. "What happened?"

I looked up at Mr. Fetlock. I had no idea what to say.

"I . . . er . . . I . . . er . . ." I tried desperately to think of a likely story, but my mind was a blank.

"He sat on one," said Mr. Fetlock quickly. "I mean, he, er, sort of stepped on it and . . . Actually he doesn't like to talk about it, do you, Harry?"

"No," I said quickly. "I don't."

Ed was still looking at me, and although he

said nothing further, I could tell that he was very suspicious. But fortunately, or rather, unfortunately, his attention was distracted by what was happening on the racetrack. Several of the horses had collided with one another and fallen in a tangled heap. And at the bottom of the heap, struggling to get back on his feet, was Silver Streak.

"Oh, no!" wailed Mr. Fetlock. "That's another race lost! Where will it all end?"

Well, it certainly did not end that day. In the next race, in which Nifty Dancer was being ridden by Ted, everything went very well until the horses were going around for the second time. Then, just as Nifty Dancer was coming up into second place, he reared and threw Ted to the ground. The jockey was unhurt, but that was the end of the race for Nifty Dancer.

"I'll be a ruined man at this rate," said Mr. Fetlock, holding his brow. "It just isn't fair!"

Then came the final race, and with my heart in my mouth I watched Black Lightning being ridden out to the starting line. Ed gave us a friendly wave from the saddle, and I waved back, hoping against hope that the incident with the glue would have no ill effects on Black Lightning's performance. But just as I thought this, I saw something that shattered any hopes I might have had. Standing at the starting line, Black Lightning put up his head and gave an unmistakable yawn!

In a flash the mystery was solved. With his hooves glued to the stable floor, the poor horse had been unable to sleep all night. So now, just when he should have been at his most energetic, he was absolutely exhausted, and even *I* knew that absolutely exhausted horses never won races.

And that is exactly what happened. Black Lightning could hardly bring himself to gallop, and when he did so, it was the slowest gallop I have ever seen. The crowd around the railings began to laugh.

"Wake up!" they shouted. "It's only one o'clock!"

Mr. Fetlock turned red with embarrassment.

"I'm going back to the truck," he said. "This is all too terrible."

I walked back with him, but I was unable to say anything. Later, when Ed joined us again, I noticed that he was still looking at me very suspiciously.

A cheat exposed

We were to go to more races first thing the following day, and so I went to bed early. Thinking about the day's events kept me awake for a while, but at last I drifted off to sleep. I had bad dreams, though—dreams in which horses were running around in circles, falling over one another, whinnying in alarm. But it was not the dreams that woke me up. It was a noise.

I sat up in bed. Somewhere in the stables, somebody had dropped something, and it had fallen with a *clang*. I reached out in the darkness for the flashlight that stood on my bedside table and switched it on. Then, putting on my bathrobe and slippers, I crept as quietly as I could to my door.

There was a moon in the sky, a great silver ball that bathed the yard and the stables in a soft half-light. The shadows, though, were dark and seemed as if they could be concealing all kinds of dangers. I looked around me, and just as I did so I heard a noise again. This time it was softer, as though somebody was moving something around.

I turned off my flashlight and tiptoed quietly in the direction from which the noise was coming. There was a saddle room next to one of the horse stalls, and it seemed to me that whoever was making the noise was in there.

Slowly, I inched my way toward the door of the saddle room. It was closed, but through the cracks in the wood I could just make out the glow of a flashlight inside. I was sure of it now: whoever was inside was preparing to sabotage tomorrow's races. He was doing something to one of the saddles, perhaps, so that it would fall off in the middle of the race. The thought of it made me seethe with anger, and I was more determined than ever to see who it was and expose him to Mr. Fetlock. How proud Aunt Japonica and Aunt Thessalonika would be that I had solved my first mystery so quickly!

Then I sneezed. It was not one of those sneezes that you know are coming and that you can stop by pressing your finger against your nose. It was one of those loud ones that come out in a rush before you know where you are.

I stood stock still. The sneeze had been so loud that it couldn't have been missed by the person in the saddle room. I listened hard. Everything was quiet, but I saw the flashlight beam move inside the room, and I knew that I had to hide quickly.

I looked around me. My own room was too far away for me to run to, but there was a storeroom close by, and I could see that its door was open. Dashing across the yard, I flung myself through the storeroom door and crouched down in a far corner, hidden in the shadows.

There was the sound of a door opening outside. Then a voice came drifting across the yard. It was not much louder than a whisper, but it carried very well in the stillness of the night.

"I know you're there! And I'm going to find you!"

I shivered with fear. With its open door, the storeroom was an obvious place to hide, and the person out there, whether it was Ted, Fred, or Ed, was bound to find me.

I looked around. If only there had been a trapdoor or a large box I could crawl into. But there was nothing. The only thing I could make out properly in the moonlight coming through the window was a large pot with a brush sticking out of it.

That was it! That was the way to save myself!

The footsteps outside grew louder. Now they were right outside the storeroom door. Then the beam of the flashlight appeared and flashed across the room. At first it missed me, but when it came back for its second swing, there I was, crouched down, caught square in the beam of light.

"So!" said the voice. "It's you! I knew there was something funny about you from the beginning. You're not a jockey, but a spy!"

I was too terrified to say anything.

"Well, well!" said the person at the door. Slowly he began to walk toward me.

He stopped.

"What . . . what?" came a puzzled voice. And then, *squelch*, *squelch*, *squelch*, and silence.

"What's going on?" said the voice angrily. "What have you done?"

I knew that it was safe for me to get up, so I leapt to my feet and ran across to the light switch. As the light came on, all was revealed. There was a pair of boots firmly stuck in the thick layer of glue I had spread on the floor in front of the doorway. And there, in the boots, looking trapped and flustered, was . . . Ted!

"So you're the cheat," I said, my voice sounding very disappointed. I had expected it to be Ed, or maybe even Fred; instead, it was the pleasant, smiling Ted.

Ted looked down at his boots.

"Aren't you ashamed of yourself?" I said sharply. "Poor Mr. Fetlock doesn't deserve what you've been doing to him."

Ted still hung his head.

"I know," he said. "It's been very bad of me. But they forced me to do it."

"They?" I asked. "Who are *they*?"

"The League of Cheats," said Ted sadly. "They found me cheating just a tiny bit once. I normally never cheat, and I don't know why I did that time. Anyway, they told me if I didn't join them, they'd tell everybody about my cheating, and I'd be ruined."

I looked at the jockey. A tear was running down his right cheek, and I felt very sorry for him.

"Don't worry," I said. "I'll explain it to Mr. Fetlock and ask him not to be too severe with you."

Ted lifted his face and beamed with pleasure.

"Oh, thank you," he said. "Thank you so much."

"But in return," I went on, "you must tell me all about the League of Cheats and help us to put a stop to their cheating. Will you do that?"

Ted looked a bit worried, but he knew that he had to agree.

"I could try," he said.

I moved over to him and began to help him out of the boots, which were firmly stuck to the floor.

"Good," I said. "Now you tell me everything you know, and we can work out a plan."

Ted told me everything he knew about the League of Cheats. It was run, he said, by a man he had never seen, a man called Charlie Heat. He was the Chief Cheat, and he arranged cheating all over the place. But it was impossible to find him by yourself. What you had to do was to be seen by one of his men to be a good cheat, and then they would ask you to join. If you cheated very well, you might be taken to meet Charlie Heat.

"So," said Ted, smiling as the idea came to him, "why don't we arrange for *you* to cheat at the races tomorrow and see what happens?"

It was a good idea, but there was something that worried me. Ted's plan meant that I would have to ride a racehorse, and not only that, it involved a very, very uncomfortable end. But I had no alternative. I was determined to put an end to the League of Cheats, and if this meant that I had to take risks, then I would be happy to do just that.

The Water Jump

The racetrack was already crowded by the time we arrived. I looked at the faces of the crowd, hoping to see my aunts, but there was still no sign of them. I was longing to be able to tell them of the plan that Ted and I had hatched, and to find out what they thought of it.

We saddled the horses and led them to the pen where the jockeys were preparing to mount. Mr. Fetlock stayed behind at the rail, where he was talking to a friend. From time to time, he glanced nervously at Black Lightning, wondering whether his favorite racehorse would let him down again.

"Are you ready?" Ted whispered to me. "Are you sure you still want to go ahead with it?"

"Yes," I replied under my breath, trying not to sound too nervous. I was ready, and I did want to go ahead with it, but part of me was wishing that I had never agreed to the plan.

"All right," said Ted. "I'll give you a leg up."

And with that I found myself being hoisted up and onto Black Lightning's back. It all happened very quickly, and before I knew where I was, I had the reins in my hand and Black Lightning had joined the cluster of horses making their way toward the starting gate.

"Good luck!" Ted called out. "Remember to hold on tight!"

I gritted my teeth and concentrated on staying in the saddle. Although Black Lightning was only walking, there was a spring in his step that worried me. Would I be able to hold on for more than a few moments once the race started? I doubted it.

We reached the starting gate, where the starters led each horse into the squashed little boxes that allowed everybody to charge off at the same time. I could tell that Black Lightning was excited by the way he pawed at the ground, and I wished that he was as tired as he had been the previous day.

"Are you ready?" called out one of the starters. Then the starting pistol rang out, the doors of the starting gates fell open, and there in front of us stretched the racetrack with its jumps.

Black Lightning gave a leap, which took me completely by surprise. For a moment it seemed as if we were both in the air, but then I felt the thud of his galloping hooves against the turf. I shot up and down in the saddle, holding onto the reins with one hand and desperately trying to keep myself on Black Lightning with the other.

I had little chance to look around me, but I'm sure that I saw Mr. Fetlock's face flashing past me at the rail. His mouth was open with

surprise, and I think he shouted out something, but I was soon past him.

I looked ahead. It was a miracle that I was
still on Black Lightning at all, and now we
were coming up to the first jump. It seemed
very high—far too high to get over—but Black
Lightning's ears were flattened against his
head, and he seemed determined to clear it.

With a great leap, the racehorse launched
himself into the air. I saw the top of the jump
passing below me, and I felt the air rushing
past in a cool torrent. And then, having gone
as high as he could go, Black Lightning began
to sink back to the earth beneath him.

I didn't. As the horse went down, I stayed
up, and when I next looked, the saddle was no
longer below me. There was nothing but the
wide pond of water that always comes after
the water jump.

I closed my eyes. Down I tumbled, down
toward the waiting water, and then, with a
splash, I was in it. The water broke my fall, of
course, and I was unhurt, but there I was,
sitting in the middle of the pond, covered in

muddy water with the other horses and jockeys flying over my head. I felt very foolish, but at the same time I was very pleased indeed that the race was over as far as I was concerned.

"Well done!" said Ted as he came out to collect me and to lead me back to the saddling pen. "Everybody thinks you fell off deliberately."

"I didn't!" I said. "I was going to fall off a bit later, on some nice, soft grass."

"That doesn't matter," Ted went on. "*They* think you meant to fall off, so that Black Lightning would not win. In fact, here comes one of them now."

I looked behind me. There was a rather dishonest-looking man coming over. He smiled at me and passed me a clean white handkerchief.

"Mop your face with that," he said. "That was a very clever fall."

"Thank you," I said. "It took a lot of practice to get it just right."

He nodded. "We like to see cheating as good as that." He glanced over his shoulder. Ted had melted away and there was nobody else around. "In fact, would you be interested in meeting somebody who could help you with your cheating?"

My heart gave a leap. This was it! This was the invitation that would enable me to expose the League of Cheats.

"I would," I said eagerly.

"Then come with me," the man said, nodding in the direction of the other end of the racetrack. "I'll take you to the boss."

charlie Heat

We struggled through the crowd of race-goers, the dishonest-looking man leading the way. Some of the people recognized me as the jockey who had ridden Black Lightning and fallen off so quickly. One or two of them muttered something under their breath, and another hissed "Cheat" as I walked past.

There were several cars and trucks parked at the end of the racetrack. Here and there, groups of men were standing around, talking to one another or unsaddling horses. My companion approached one of these groups, telling me to wait until he called me over. I stood where I was, watching while he spoke briefly to a rather fat figure in a white suit. As he did so, this man looked over in my direction and then nodded. With a wave of the hand I was beckoned over.

I walked toward them slowly, my heart beating like a hammer within me. I had succeeded in getting right to the heart of the League of Cheats, but what now? Ted had promised that he would arrive with Mr. Fetlock, but where were they? Did he expect me to challenge Charlie Heat myself?

The fat man was looking hard at me.

"I saw your fall," he said. "It was a good piece of cheating, very good."

I looked at his eyes. They were like the eyes of a snake, small and bright, and very, very sly. Even if I did not know who he was, I would have distrusted him immediately. There was something about him that was frightening. He was the sort of person you met in nightmares, the sort of person who made you wake up with the sharp taste of fear in your mouth.

"I could use your help," he went on, his eyes still boring into me. "I could find work for you."

I pretended not to understand. "What sort of work?" I asked. "Would it be with horses?"

Charlie Heat smiled. "Horses could come into it," he said. "But there'd be other things too. There are all kinds of things to cheat in, you know: running competitions, jumping competitions, quiz shows, dog shows, cat shows. In fact, anything at all."

I listened to him in astonishment. What possible reason could there be for cheating on such a scale? Was he crazy? Perhaps that was the answer: perhaps Charlie Heat was a madman after all.

I decided to find out directly.

"But how do you manage to cheat in all those things?" I asked.

As I asked my question, Charlie Heat's eyes began to glow, and he started to shake as he gave his answer.

"It's because of *them*!" he said. "All those

so-called honest people! Oh, I could tell you a thing or two! I could tell you about the time I sabotaged a dog show by slipping in a cat disguised as a dog. The dogs went wild! You've never seen such a scene. It totally ruined the show!''

He laughed out loud, a horrible, sneering laugh. Then he went on, ''And then there was the time my buddy Billy entered a swimming contest and I had my people secretly sew lead weights into the swimsuits of the other competitors. Oh, that was a treat! It was all they could do to keep afloat, let alone swim fast. My friend won by six lengths, he did! Six lengths!''

''But why do you like cheating so much?'' The question slipped out without my thinking.

He looked at me as if he was puzzled that anybody could ask such a silly thing.

''Why do I like cheating?'' he asked. ''As I told you, it's because of *them*—those snivelling, sneaky, 'Aren't I better than you?' honest people. *They* accused me of cheating when I was a little boy, and I shall never forgive them for it. I vowed to make them pay for it, and I certainly have!''

''And did you cheat when you were a boy?'' I asked.

''Of course I did,'' snapped Charlie Heat. ''Who wouldn't?''

For a moment I said nothing. Then I could contain myself no longer.

''I wouldn't!'' I shouted. ''I think cheating's a terrible thing to do. And I would never, never work for you and your League of Cheats!''

There! I had said it. But what would happen now?

His eyes opened wide, and I could tell that I had surprised him.

''Who told you about the League of Cheats?'' he asked icily.

I took a deep breath. It was no use waiting for Ted and Mr. Fetlock now. I would have to be brave.

''I know all about you,'' I said. ''You're Charlie Heat, president of the League of

Cheats. You've been cheating Mr. Fetlock and lots of other people too. And we're going to show you up for what you are!"

Charlie Heat's eyes narrowed again, and he took a quick step forward. Then, in a sudden swoop, he grabbed the lapels of my jacket and lifted me up in the air.

"Oh, yes?" he said menacingly. "And who's going to believe you?"

I opened my mouth to reply, but no sound came out. I was so frightened that my tongue seemed to have stuck to the top of my mouth. I tried to wriggle free, but Charlie Heat's grip was too tight, and I only found myself more firmly trapped. Then, just when I thought that all was lost, I heard a voice from behind us.

"I'll believe her!" the voice cried.

Charlie Heat spun around, still holding me in midair. There was nobody there—nobody, that is, apart from a strange-looking black-and-white horse.

"What was that?" shouted Charlie Heat.

"I said, I'll believe her, Mr. Heat! Your

cheating days are over!" the voice said again.

I could hardly believe it, but there was only one explanation. The horse was talking.

Charlie was so astonished that he let me drop with a thump.

"I . . . I . . . ," he stuttered.

The horse took a few steps forward, and as it did so I realized that I knew its voice. It was Aunt Japonica in another of her brilliant disguises.

Charlie Heat, though, did not know this, and he turned pale with fear. Then, turning on his heels, he shot off down the racetrack, squealing with fright.

"Quick!" said Aunt Japonica from within her horse costume. "Jump on."

I looked at the horse's back. It looked rather bumpy and uncomfortable, but I did as I was told.

"Ow!" came Aunt Thessalonika's voice from behind me. "Careful where you put your feet."

"Off we go," called Aunt Japonica from

the front, and off we went, with Aunt Japonica as the front legs and Aunt Thessalonika as the back. It was not a smooth ride, but it was certainly safer than Black Lightning.

Charlie Heat could not run very fast, and we were gaining on him. Ahead of us, though, was a large jump, and I wondered how he would deal with this. Surely that would stop him long enough for us to catch up with him.

"We've got him now," panted Aunt Japonica. "He'll never be able to get over that jump."

I thought so too, but just at that moment, the running figure of Charlie Heat swerved to one side and went *around* the jump!

"Look at that!" shouted Aunt Japonica in indignation. "What a cheat!"

We galloped, or rather my aunts galloped, all the quicker, so angry were they with Charlie Heat's behavior. We were now approaching the jump ourselves, and at any moment I expected my aunts to swerve and follow Charlie Heat around the side of the jump. But no. My aunts would never cheat, and with a great leap, the aunt-filled horse, with me on its back, sailed into the air and over the jump. For a terrible moment I thought I would fall again, just as I had done when Black Lightning launched himself over the jump, but somehow I managed to hang on. Then, with a thump, we landed and galloped away after the now very tired Charlie Heat.

Within minutes we had caught up with him. He was so tired and frightened, he could run no more.

"I give up! I give up!" he squealed as he collapsed to the ground, his white suit covered with mud.

I climbed down, and Aunt Japonica soon appeared from the front of the horse outfit. With a little struggling and pushing, both aunts had soon worked themselves free, and the outfit lay limp on the ground. There was shouting in the distance, and to my relief I saw Mr. Fetlock, together with Ed, Ted, and Fred, running over the grass to join us.

"Here's the cheat," said Aunt Japonica, pointing at the wretched Charlie Heat.

"Well done!" cried Mr. Fetlock, beaming with pleasure.

"Don't congratulate us," said Aunt Thessalonika modestly. "It's Harriet Bean who deserves the praise."

Mr. Fetlock warmly shook my hand, as did the jockeys. Then, while the men led Charlie Heat off for a little talk with the racetrack police, I helped my two detective aunts roll up their horse outfit and carry it back to Mr. Fetlock's truck.

"That was a very clever plan," said Aunt Japonica. "We had suspected Charlie Heat for some time, and this proved that our suspicions were right."

I was puzzled. "But why did you suspect him?" I asked.

Aunt Japonica laughed. "It was simple," she said. "Look at his name. There's a strong clue there."

I thought of his name. Charlie Heat. Mr. Heat. Mr. C. Heat. C. Heat. Cheat!

"I see," I said, laughing. "That was a very good clue."

"Yes," said Aunt Japonica. "Sometimes names tell us a great deal. Did I ever tell you about how we caught a famous thief purely because I thought there was something funny about his name?"

"Oh, yes," chipped in Aunt Thessalonika. "The case of Mr. R. O'Ber. That was a very interesting case."

But there was no time for my aunts to tell me about it that day, as we had now arrived back at the truck and we could see that Mr. Fetlock had set up some sort of party to celebrate the end of the League of Cheats. There were delicious-looking cakes set out on a folding table and all sorts of wonderful sandwiches.

We had a very good feast. Even Black Lightning enjoyed himself and ate six cucumber sandwiches in one mouthful.

"A good mystery is always best when it's over," said Aunt Japonica as she licked the cream off her fingers.

"I agree," said Aunt Thessalonika, her mouth full of sandwich.

"And so do I," I said.

Don't miss any adventure, mystery, and fun with these Alexander McCall Smith titles!

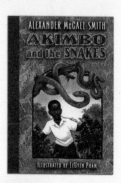

Now available in paperback!

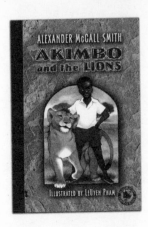

A NOTE ON THE AUTHOR

ALEXANDER MCCALL SMITH has written more than fifty books, including the *New York Times* bestselling No. 1 Ladies' Detective Agency mysteries and The Sunday Philosophy Club series. A professor of medical law at Edinburgh University, he was born in what is now Zimbabwe and taught law at the University of Botswana. He lives in Edinburgh, Scotland.

Visit him at WWW.ALEXANDERMCCALLSMITH.COM

A NOTE ON THE ILLUSTRATOR

LAURA RANKIN is also the illustrator of the picture books *Rabbit Ears*, *Swan Harbor*, and *The Handmade Alphabet*. She lives in Maine.